This book belongs to

....

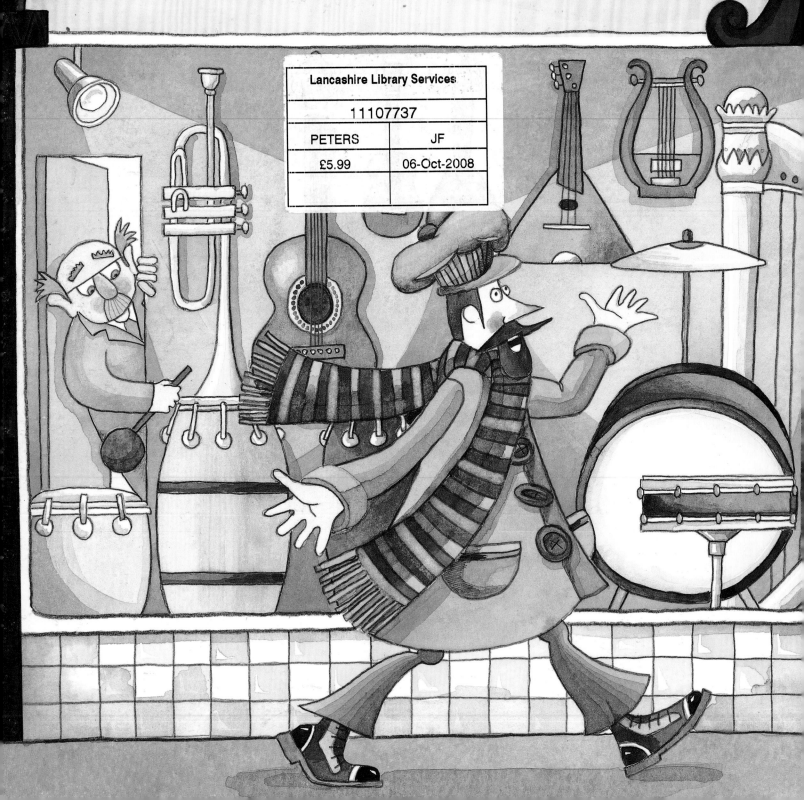

Do you do a Didgeridoo?

Written by Nick Page

Open

Illustrations by Sara Baker

Hello, Mr Music-man, how do you do?
Do you do a didgeridoo?
One that blows a low wa-hoo?
So, do you do a didgeridoo?

Do you do a didgeridoo?
One that blows a low wa-hoo?
I'd paint it in purple, or yellow, or blue;
I could paint it in every kind of hue!
I'd even play one you can see right through!
So, do you do a didgeridoo?

Splat!

No.
We didgeridon't.

11

Do you do a didgeridoo?
One that blows a low wa-hoo?
Oh, Mr Music-man, tell me true!
I want to duet with my best friend, Sue,
This very musical kangaroo.
I've brought all my friends from down at the zoo,
To ask you to make my dreams come true.
So do you do a didgeridoo?

Do you do a didgeridoo?
One that blows a low wa-hoo?
I could imitate bird sounds just for you!
I could make it squawk like a cockatoo,
Or imitate the pigeon's 'coo',
Or the plaintive cry of a lone curlew,
Or sound like an owl – 'tu-whit, tu-whoo' –
Or the angry grunt of an old emu,
As it mourns the fact that it never flew.
But tell me, please, oh tell me, do,
Do you do a didgeridoo?

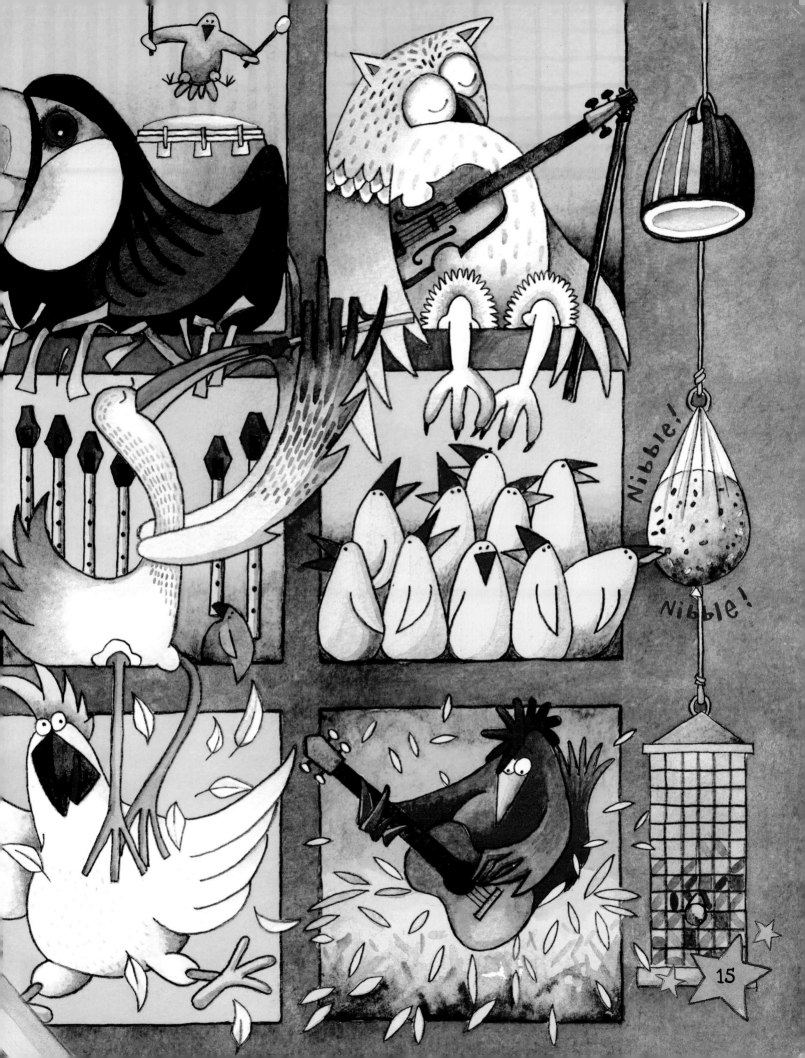

Do you do a didgeridoo?
One that blows a low wa-hoo?
I've searched from here to Timbuktu,
I've been to Rome and to Peru,
I played in a band with a tiny shrew,
A caribou and a mad gnu.
We played the blues on the old kazoo.
Some people called it a hullabaloo!
But now I want to play something new.
So do you do a didgeridoo?

We love the Moody Gnus

19

So do you do a didgeridoo?
One that blows a low wa-hoo?
I could serenade guests at a barbecue,
Or play for somebody cooking a stew,
(Or Italians eating tiramisu,
Or Indians cooking sag aloo.)
Or play for barbers as they shampoo,
Or sailors getting a new tattoo,
If you don't have one, then it's adieu,
Goodbye, farewell, and toodle-oo
So Mr Music-man, let's review:
Do you do a didgeridoo?

No. We didgeridon't.

So do you do a didgeridoo?
One that blows a low wa-hoo?
I'll take it away with me, that's what I'll do!
I could play it while paddling in my canoe,
Or sauntering down the avenue,
Or shivering in my small igloo,
Or staying in teepees among the Sioux.
So please, Mr Music-man, tell me true:
Do you do a didgeridoo?
Oh do, please, tell me, tell me, do –
DO YOU DO A DIDGERIDOO?

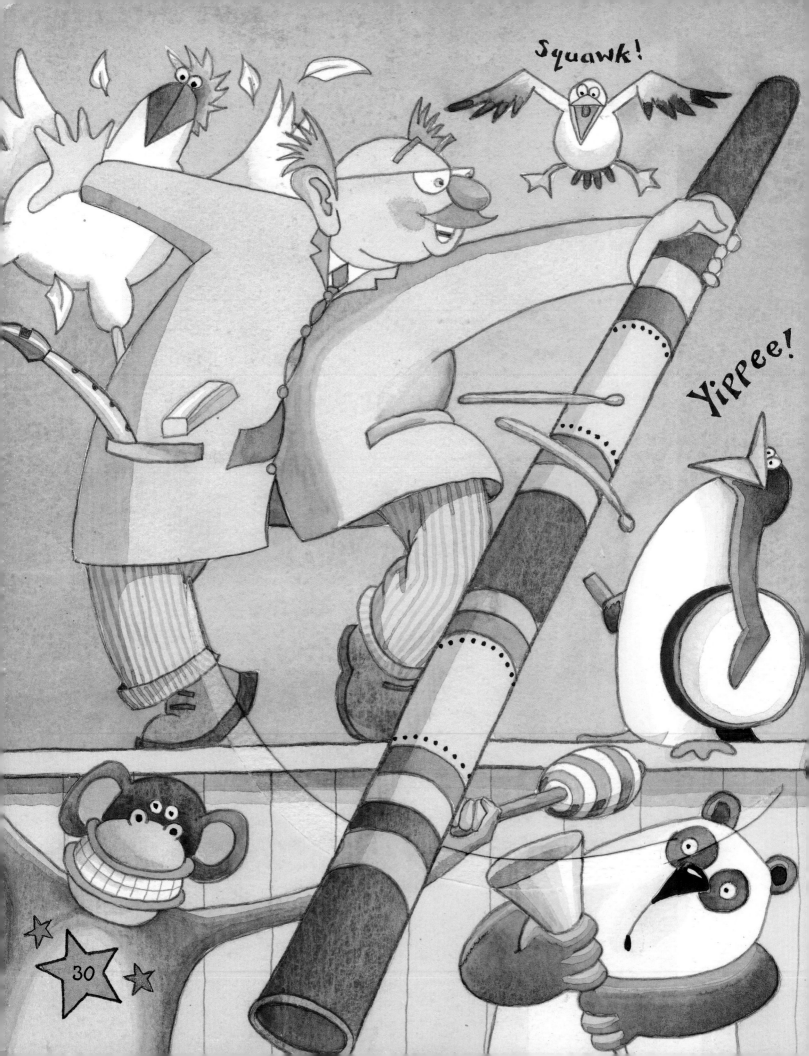

YES, WE DO A DIDGERIDOO!
Look, Mr Customer, just for you!
You can paint it in purple or yellow or blue,
You can play a duet with the kangaroo, Sue,
You can serenade everyone down at the zoo,
You can play it while paddling in your canoe,
You can play in Peru or in Timbuktu,
You can play it instead of your old kazoo,
You can play by the side of the barbecue,
With the shrew, the gnu and the caribou.
And listen! It blows a low wa-hoo!

Boom!

Boom!

So yes, we do a didgeridoo.
What do you want: just one, or two?
And shall I wrap it up for you?

Actually...

. . . I've changed
my mind!

37